Pull up a Log

Guest Editorial by Jo Ross–Barrett

Welcome to the disabled and/or neurodivergent people's edition of *Shoreline of Infinity*! I know that name is a little long, but I really wanted to make it clear from the beginning that this edition is ours. It was an incredible experience to read through so many fascinating submissions by people from our communities – I hope you will enjoy the selection of pieces in this issue as much as I do. There were more excellent contributions than could be crammed into a single edition, so you may find more writing from disabled and/or neurodivergent writers in upcoming issues of Shoreline of Infinity too.

I tried to ensure a variety of themes throughout this issue when selecting pieces. While my guidelines welcomed any works with a focus on sci-fi (perhaps with a dash of fantasy or speculative elements), as long as the creator identified as disabled and/or neurodivergent, I also made a list of some of the themes that often weigh on my mind with regards to our experiences as communities to see if it would spark any ideas for writers out there. In these pages you will find diverse examples of disabled and/or neurodivergent perspectives, musings on our representation in media and fierce stories on disability justice in different contexts, in addition to a couple of stories without a heavy focus on these aspects of identity. There's a page of content notes too, which I recommend checking out before going through the rest of the issue – from toxic relationships and casual ableism to medical trauma and eugenics, this edition spans a lot of topics that negatively affect the disabled and neurodivergent community in all-too-familiar ways.

Two of the stories are told in Scots: *How Yer Glaikit Gran Beat Back the Beat* by Callum Dougan and *The Alien Invasion* by Ely Percy. I was delighted to see these lively, funny and imaginative pieces in the Shoreline inbox and I'm excited to share them with as wide an audience as possible. This magazine is published in Scotland for the Universe and I wanted to do that justice by showcasing some of the rich linguistic varieties that our literature has to offer. As a New Scot who grew up in South Wales, I came to Scotland aged eighteen with no working knowledge of Scots varieties – though I had to learn quickly while studying Scottish literature! If you aren't familiar with Scots works, the best advice I was ever given when I started reading them was to read the piece aloud to myself – I suggest you do the same if you can. Whether you're a native speaker or a total newcomer to Scots, I hope you enjoy these wonderful stories.

As an autistic non-binary person who loves sci-fi and fantasy, I've had a long-term conflicted feeling about robots, aliens and fantastical non-human creatures being my primary sources of representation for both neurotype and gender. On the one hand, inauthentic but supposedly realist portrayals of humans like me can be just as harmful (if not more so)... but on the other hand there is something deeply unsettling about the idea that many members

ISSUE 28: NOVEMBER 2021

Disabled and neurodivergent people's issue

**Award-winning science fiction magazine
published in Scotland for the Universe.**

ISSN 2059-2590

ISBN 978-1-7396736-1-1

Submissions of fiction, art, reviews, poetry, non-fiction are
welcomed: visit the website to find out how to submit.

www.shorelineofinfinity.com

Publisher
Shoreline of Infinity Publications / The New Curiosity Shop
Edinburgh
Scotland

250422

Cover art: Cameron Ax

Contents

Editorial Team

Guest Editor: Jo Ross-Barrett

Co-founder, Editor-in-Chief, Editor: Noel Chidwick

Co-founder: Mark Toner

Deputy Editor & Poetry Editor: Russell Jones

Reviews Editor: Samantha Dolan

Non-fiction Editor: Pippa Goldschmidt

Art Director (Acting): Caroline Grebbell

Copy-editors: Pippa Goldschmidt, Russell Jones, Iain Maloney, Eris Young

Special thanks to Thomas Clark for editing the stories written in Scots

Proof Reader: Cat Hellisen

Fiction Consultant: Eric Brown

First Contact

www.shorelineofinfinity.com

contact@shorelineofinfinity.com

Twitter: @shoreinf

of more privileged groups perceive people like me as 'other' to the extent of not being human. However, when someone from the autistic community chooses to reclaim this trope and use it to discuss the feelings that stem from marginalisation due to these differences, all I feel is bright, powerful joy. A. P. Slevin's *I Landed Here* is a poem that resonated with me deeply. One stanza in particular sums up the frustrations and hypocrisies that often surround masking (attempting to hide neurodivergent traits for the sake of being accepted and/or safe):

> *They tell you that*
> *They like you*
> *As you, but only when*
> *You're like them.*

My greatest hope for this edition of Shoreline of Infinity is that it will help all kinds of readers to better understand and empathise with the wide variety of uniquely disabled and/or neurodivergent perspectives out there, especially if they're not like you. At any rate, editing it has certainly given me a lot to think about and I hope you will find the resulting issue thought-provoking too.

For content notes, please turn to page 81

Our Guest Editor, **Jo Ross-Barrett** (they/them), is an experienced writer, editor and inclusion consultant. They are also a queer autistic non-binary person with depression and anxiety. Jo has a Distinction-grade MSc in Publishing; Their writing has been published in two anthologies by Monstrous Regiment – The Bi-ble (Volume 1) and So Hormonal – as well as in AZE Journal (an online magazine for aromantic-spectrum, asexual-spectrum and agender people), We Are Here (a collection of poetry by LGBTQIA+ disabled and chronically ill people), Sapphic Writers' Zine and Coin-Operated Press.

The Apology
M. Shaw

Today's apology, we have been told, is going to be nothing short of sublime. Tear-jerker. Edge of your seat. The columnists have pulled out all the stock phrases. Feel good hit of the summer, probably. Anyway, it's going to be the best apology yet. Which is a hell of a goal to set, given the amount of competition it has from the many, many apologies that have come before.

Jon and I talk about this during the 90-minute drive to work. It's not a fun or interesting discussion, but, after only four years of marriage, we already lack much in the way of other things to talk about. I imagine any two people in the world have a set lifetime limit of interesting conversation that is possible between them before it all settles into repetitive small talk, retelling of the relationship's more interesting past, bickering, and silence. People tell me this is just what marriage is like: a pattern that you

Art: piyaphun

become stuck in, often for the rest of your life; able to identify its problems but unable to imagine any alternative. I tend to feel sorry for people who believe this, until I realize I'm one of them.

We ask each other what we think the apology will be like, compare notes about some of the other ones, eventually agree that we're tired of hearing about it. Our attempt to cope with the routine mediocrity of the day-to-day is, itself, a mediocre routine.

"I liked the old CEO's apologies better," Jon admits. "They were funnier. I liked how he rolled around on the floor. He actually tore his jacket all down the back one time, remember?"

"You mean Wagner?" I catch Jon's look. "Relax, the car isn't bugged. We both have great disciplinary records, we're nowhere near the company's radar for that kind of thing." This would change very quickly if any of our coworkers interested in getting snitch bonuses caught us saying the name aloud, but those people aren't here.

"If I were comfortable with it being said, I would have said it first," says Jon.

Names of disgraced executives are something you're supposed to keep to yourself. Which isn't entirely unhealthy. Everyone needs to have things that they keep to themselves, so that the novelty doesn't wear out the way it does with everything we do talk about. I, for example, often daydream about doing horrifying violence to many of the people I know. I can't help doing it, but it's fine. It's not like I would ever really do any of it. I've never told anyone this, even Jon; it's a little something, just for me.

I try to return the conversation to its former track. "I do remember when he tore his jacket, though. *Fat guuuuy in a liiiiittle coat!*" I say, mimicking two weeks' worth of memes from four years ago. It gets a chuckle out of Jon. Of course, the real joke here is that the idea of a person being fat is not funny, and the idea of a person wearing clothes the wrong size is, at best, slightly funny, and yet this phrase, repeated so endlessly in office break rooms that it still echoes in our car now, is comedy gold. "It's true," I say. "Barnard doesn't use enough physical comedy."

"No, he just gets other people to do it for him," says Jon. "I mean, we all know that board member having a heart attack in the middle of the last one was staged, right?"

"Oh, totally. He was out of the hospital in two days. Probably playing *Call of Duty* the whole time."

And with that, we are absorbed in silence. The mistake I've made here is not disagreeing with anything. I have provided no avenues for me or Jon to try to prove ourselves right, thus prolonging the conversation. *Obviously* the board member was faking his heart attack. We and all of our Facebook friends have already agreed to this multiple times, right down to the *Call of Duty* detail, all of which is very funny, because the idea of someone being able to spend two days in the hospital to take a vacation instead of lose their job and fall deeply and irrevocably into debt is outlandish for people like us. It's as cliche as observing that the CEO's name can be rotated to *DURRnard*, if you're down for a little light ableism. I should have dissented.

"Of course, it could have been just a minor heart attack," I offer, but it's too late. I get nothing out of Jon, who stares intently out the window, as if there were anything out there besides more traffic. We haven't even hit the shantytowns yet.

I-70 lies prostrate before us, its surface mirage-like through the exhaust of a hundred thousand commuters. The company has paid to have all the highways widened at least twice, to accommodate the employees at the Aurora distribution center commuting from Limon, or Fairplay, or the Mount 402 settlements. Places where we can afford housing. It's still barely enough. Add an accident or two into the mix and we'll all be late, which is something that our pace today has me deeply nervous of. I know Jon feels it too, and that we are both conscientiously not talking about it. Too stressful. Nothing we can do.

To fill the silence, I turn on the radio. They're talking, of course, about the apology. This is supposed to be a music station, but they discuss current events on the morning show, interspersed with jokes about Chris and Hounddog's (the two male hosts) wives, punctuated by goofy sound effects.

Chris and Hounddog are two of the people I like to fantasize about hurting. I don't know what they look like, but I imagine them with short beards, bright button-ups, chubby hands. Guys who look like they used to be on children's TV shows, got fired, and never quite let go. I think of coming up behind them while they're on the air, and choking them, wrapping a forearm around each of their throats. I imagine their limbs flailing as they struggle, unsuccessfully, to get free. They've never done anything to me, but these aren't revenge fantasies. It's unadulterated cruelty, purely for the fun of it. It's just a daydream.

There is also a female host, Jill, but her main purpose is yelling, "It's a legitimate question!" in follow-up to the many clearly foolish and not-legitimate questions she asks, followed by the recorded sound of a parrot squawking.

"So everyone at that huge warehouse is gonna have to stop whatever they're doing, in the middle of the work day," the voice of Chris says, clownishly, "and they're all gonna look up at these huge TV screens, just like, what's he gonna [bleep] up this time?"

It's strange to think of the CEO's apology being material for a morning show that mostly focuses on dick jokes and stories of people humiliating themselves on the internet. But this is what the apologies have become. Entertainment. Like a football game. They have pre-game and post-game analysis, highlight reels, 24-hour coverage. Bars advertise always having them on the TVs, whether it's Barnard or some other company's guy. That the apology doesn't fix what he's done, and the fact that he'll do it again, are part of the charm. It's an emotional outlet for people. Not anything serious or binding.

"You used to work at that warehouse, didn't you, Chris?" Jill interjects between the men's chuckles.

"Who hasn't!" says Chris. "We've all been in one of them, that's how we all know how it goes."

"I know how it goes because I watch it on my phone in the break room here," says Hounddog.

"Yep. Me too," says Jill.

"I mean, yes, we all do that *now*," says Chris.

"Look, don't let us hold you up," says Hounddog. "We know you need to get back to your shift sticking labels on boxes."

The joke is that most people in the Denver area *have* worked at one of the big warehouses at one time or another, and that everyone, whether they work there or not, depends on them hiring people to do things like stick labels on boxes for a wage that you have to live 90 miles away to live off of. It's a very funny joke, because we're all in on it.

"Don't worry," Hounddog continues, "we won't tell *DURRnard* you were here." They play a clip of the CEO stumbling over his words during an interview in Porky Pig-like fashion, eventually settling on *We don't allow activities such as water or other materials in the workplace* as the phrasing he's looking for, which is funny because we all live 5,200 feet above sea level and are constantly dehydrated and can't have drinks while we're on the clock.

I ask Jon, "Do you even remember what this apology is for?" No response. He's biting his nails, watching traffic move ever slower. There must be an accident ahead. I try to hold out hope. Maybe, if they get it cleaned up quick, we'll only get our employee discount turned off for a week. Living off instant beans and rice won't kill us after that long.

The morning show hosts continue to speculate about the apology. How long it will be, how hard it will be for the CEO to get through it, what a release it will be for those affected.

"Wait," Jill cuts in, "are we talking about a boner now?" They allow a moment of dead air for silent disbelief. "What? It's a legitimate question!" Sound of a parrot squawking.

"Gross," I mutter.

Jon reaches across the console and punches the stereo's power button. Chris and Hounddog's laughter cuts out, mid-guffaw. "Gross?" he repeats. I keep my eyes resolutely fixed on the stagnating flow of traffic.

Even though he only said the one word, he intoned it in just the right dramatic, minor-key fashion that I already know I'm in trouble. I should have seen this coming; I haven't been in trouble in a while, so we're due for one of these, and we've had them often enough that I can already tell where it's headed.

What's going on here is that he's going to play this like I meant *his* boner is gross. I'm fairly sure he doesn't actually believe that I meant this. Jon *is* hypersensitive about his penis, which he blames on an ex who shamed him about its smell, and on his parents for reasons he doesn't talk about. But this doesn't feel like that. The timing of the remark feels scripted, like a movie. Which, to an extent, it is, given how many times we've retread this same scenario at home. Like the apologies, it's a thing that repeats. We seem to settle it each time, only to have it pop up again somewhere down the road.

I steal a glance at Jon and realize that he's doing exactly what I was doing a few minutes ago. He's trying to stimulate the conversation. It's understandable, in a way. Neither of us wants to think about being late to work, getting a tic on our disciplinary records, getting our discount cut or, worse, getting our purchase account suspended and not being able to buy anything at all for a while. This is just his idea of more pleasant thoughts.

If it matters, Jon doesn't smell great down there, and he's not exempt from the list of people I like to imagine hurting badly. Sometimes I imagine tying him to a chair and pulling on his foreskin. Not in a sexy way. Really pulling it back, over and over, like a rubber band I'm about to flick off my finger. Sometimes I imagine doing this until I pull it right off. *Fwoosh*. Like a sock. Sometimes, in my imagination, I stuff an actual sock in his mouth before doing this, and sometimes I let him scream. Not in real life, of course. I would never actually do any of this.

I look into the distance, through the space between my hands on the steering wheel, and realize that this has become my life. This thing Jon's doing, this is far from new. The argument is just another form of entertainment. We've done it a thousand times before, and while I've never exactly initiated it, I've always gone along with it. What's the alternative? At least we're only pretending to hate each other, instead of actually hating each other, right?

Maybe it's the atmosphere this time. The highway off-gassing around us, the car smelling from one too many drive-thru breakfast bags crumpled up and thrown in the back seat. Something makes me feel like this thing we're doing is what I really meant when I said "gross," not anything to do with the radio.

So, here is where I would normally say, "You know I didn't mean you," or something else that we would pretend, for the sake of civility, isn't so obvious. But I don't. Instead, I let one hand venture off the steering wheel and turn the radio back on. I don't look at Jon's face.

The men's laughter is just dying out, meaning that we have missed functionally nothing, besides the first part of a joke that now concludes with one of them saying, "Just the tip," twice.

"Wasn't the last apology about the exact same thing anyway?" says Hounddog.

"No, it was about money," Chris groans. They play the *ka-ching* sound of a cash register in the background. The joke here is that they're making it sound like a trifle among people who always want more, when actually Barnard's last apology was about our paychecks failing to hit our accounts for the entire month of December. It's funny because we're all employed, so what are we complaining about? We got our back pay in the middle of January and the apology came at the beginning of March (after a three-week delay due to "scheduling conflicts"). Anyone still complaining about it by that point was dismissed as entitled, bitter, holding a grudge. The company's stock value went up afterwards. Wages didn't.

Back then, I even caught myself rolling my eyes when it came up. I had just wanted the whole matter to be over after a month-long struggle to make ends meet, and another month-long struggle to get the electricity and internet turned back on. I knew, in the moment, that this had been the whole point: to wear us down until we just wanted to get through it. Even if there was no justice or vindication for us. Even if we knew it would happen again.

I still avoid looking at Jon, but I can feel the cold seething off him in the passenger seat. He's waiting for his moment, now, too. He'll stay quiet just long enough to make me feel like I've dodged the argument, and then he'll launch right back in.

The radio hosts are making fun of Barnard and his apologies now, but in a way where they're also making excuses for him. They talk about his youth and inexperience in the role of CEO and play sounds of babies whining (he's 48 and has held the job for two years), they complain about union rules and play sounds of people snoring while a boss grumbles in the background (we don't have a union), they wonder at how convoluted the law can be around these kinds of things (paying your employees isn't complicated), make fun of Barnard's hair and neckties, accompanied by slide whistle sounds, and then devolve into fart jokes.

Jon finds his moment and turns the radio back off. "No, nonono no. You cannot just drop a comment like that and try to use talk radio to dodge."

"I know you're bored, but find some other way to pass the time." I turn the radio on.

Punching the button makes me feel like my brain is shifting into a higher gear. I can't let him have this one. It's too obvious, too predictable. I can already trace the trajectory of the argument over the next few days, from my denial and the interrogation it's met with, to the resolute silence of the drive home, to the eventual weepy breakdown from Jon in which he recounts his traumas, to me begging him for forgiveness, to him begging me for forgiveness, to us both promising to do better, and then it all resets.

Only we don't do better. We'll just end up stuck in traffic again, with another fake outrage about boners. It's a conflict so outlandishly stupid that I'd feel silly even trying to describe it to anyone. It's beyond boring; it's become as unbearable as pretending to be entertained by yet another corporate apology spectacle.

Jon freezes for a moment. My gut suddenly feels like it's struggling to digest an assortment of various-sized rocks, or at least a gas station hamburger. Sweat pushes out of my pores and down my back. I need to hit the brakes. Admit I'm being a jerk, walk it back, swallow my pride and explain why my gross comment wasn't about his dick.

Except that I've seen that conversation play out before, too. I've tried these small rebellions, let myself get scared of pushing it further, and backed off, and what has it ever gotten me? More territory to backtrack over on the way to calming him down. Like the 78 miles we drive between home and work, I've got every boring, painstaking inch of it mapped out in my memory. If I stop there, I might as well have done nothing.

Incidentally, I do actually know what today's apology is about. The last time we widened I-70, the construction crews destroyed a lot of low-income housing nearby in order to do it. Sure, a sizable percentage of the people living there were technically squatting and a lot of the buildings weren't up to code, but our construction crews didn't exactly have the proper permits for demolition, there was no warning given, hundreds of families are now homeless, and some were even killed during the early morning wrecking ball salvos. Handily, this was kept out of the press until after construction was completed.

And so, our CEO will apologize to the now-homeless-or-dead people this oversight affected. Well, not *to* them. Not to their faces. On TV. In a studio, in front of an audience of shareholders, who may be Concerned about the company's Arguably Irresponsible Behavior. The apology will be full of justifications. Who could have *known* there were so many people living in those crumbling old apartments, I mean, they were practically rubble already when we found them! Who could possibly have known so many *government* permits were required to do this, I mean, the government, you know, so much red tape, always with the bureaucracy, always restricting our freedom. He was just trying to do the right thing for his company, for his employees, nay for the *world*, and yet this went so horribly wrong, and he hopes he can grow into a better CEO for it.

There will be clenched fists held in the air. Slacks-wearing knees will touch carpet. There will be tears, or, at least, the miming of wiping away tears. There will be boasting, nested in the apology, about the company, how profitable it is, all the good things it's done for commerce. There will be hilarious gaffes and meme-able soundbites. Drinking games around the occurrences of certain words will be played. He will make himself pathetic; which is to say, he will make it about him.

The shareholders will stand and applaud. They will find it in their hearts to forgive the CEO. Warm profiles of the CEO will appear in the press, with photos of him embracing his family, proclaiming this the moment he truly became a leader. Politicians will express admiration for his humility. The President himself will talk about what a great person the CEO is. Fines, citations, and lawsuits will spontaneously disappear, or quietly fail to be enforced. We will be allowed to go home 30 minutes early (without pay), urged to spend the extra time reflecting on the company's long-standing commitment to ethics and good business practices.

But not the people. Not the homeless or the dead. They will not be involved in any part of this process. We will all go through this knowing that there will be more apologies, very likely for the same scenario or something like it. We'll engage in the same old recreational cynicism, while we go on being, effectively, indentured servants of this hideous enterprise that we claim to be too smart to respect. All the relevant pull-quotes will be added to the next book of humorous apology-isms, featuring a goofy photo of the CEO's face on the cover, which will sell tens of thousands of copies through outlets that the company owns. He will look like a fool before the whole world, and nothing will change as a result.

I feel a vivid daydream coming on. It's happened before, this one. I imagine being in the room where he delivers all these apologies, rushing the stage, up between the rows of chairs, and knocking him to the ground. The pain I inflict in this one isn't as precise as the others. I'm just wailing on his prone, pillowy, business-suited form. Just kicking the shit out of him. Demanding an apology for all the things he's destroyed and stolen from my life. Screaming in his terrified face that he didn't have a permit to demolish my marriage. Not accepting whatever bullshit he stutters in response. Pounding his face until it looks like mashed potatoes. Of course, I'm not really this violent of a person. Thinking it, though, sure feels good.

Traffic is at a dead stop. I shift the car into park. Beside me, Jon's cheeks are twitching with the effort of maintaining his open-mouthed scowl. I start tabulating a mental balance sheet on how much I will pay for telling him it takes fewer muscles to smile; what names he will call me, how bad it will look when he recounts the story to others. Again, I head my mind off at the pass. I know he's going to call me those names anyway, and if he tells the story, he'll make me sound as bad as possible, no matter what I do now.

He opens his mouth.

"No," I say. "No thanks."

Every neuron in my body is rioting as I turn off the ignition and get out of the car, taking the keys with me. We're not even halfway to Aurora, and there's very little beyond the highway but the desolate Front Range, swathes of dry prairie and blighted wastes that were once farmland. I've heard stories about drifters living out here, but it's hard to tell how much of it is media sensationalism. I suppose I'm about to find out.

Behind me, Jon has gotten out of the car too. He's shouting. I don't respond. I just told him everything I need to. I keep my eyes on a fixed point on the horizon, as if I mean to walk right off the edge. I have no plan. Whatever I'm about to do will be orders of magnitude more difficult than the life I'm leaving. But the only security of that life lies in the relatively slow whittling away of possibilities. The promise that my dehumanization will happen gradually enough for me not to notice. But it's going to happen either way, and, that being the case, I might as well at least die looking for other possibilities.

Somewhere next to me, I hear the telltale click of a car door opening. Someone else is getting out of her vehicle and following behind me. With no more idea of where she's going than I do, I'm sure. I wonder what caused the traffic to stop. I dare to hope. I give myself a vision of hundreds of people on I-70 ahead of us, already doing exactly what I am doing. Of the sun setting on a highway turned into a giant, absurd parking lot in the middle of the desert, and this, I know, would be more brutal to the CEO than any physical violence anyone might ever do him.

Years later, I will wonder if this argument would have been the final nail in the coffin. If Jon could throw a stink this ridiculous and get *me* to apologize to *him* over it? In that moment, he knows, if he can get me to accept treatment this egregious, I will never have the will to break out of the pattern, as long as I live. But in the end, I'll know that there would always have been another stair for us to fall down. That the wakeup call is not so much about hitting rock bottom as it is about the moment you realize that there is no bottom. That what you allow will continue, and it will only ever grow bigger and hungrier, and there will always, somehow, be more of you to devour.

M. Shaw is graduate of the Clarion Writers' Workshop (class of 2019) and an organizer of the Denver Mercury Poetry Slam. Despite the best efforts of some, they STILL live in Arvada, Colorado, where they run the micropress Trouble Department. Their website is mshawesome.com . Their Twitter handle is @shawwillsuffice
M. Shaw is disabled — they have Complex Post-Traumatic Stress Disorder (C-PTSD)..

A Burden Eased

This Strange Dreamer

"Surprise!"

The door was barely open before Kwyatt Dreemz launched himself at Emma, thrusting his microphone under her nose. Emma knew she should scream in his face and flap her hands hysterically in the exaggerated way that budding pop stars did on the TV shows of her youth, but nothing came forth except tears.

Most surprise visits from the Content Streamaz who polluted the populace's screens resulted in an embarrassingly hysterical reaction from the surprised, but not this show. People tend to react with horror when the angel of death knocks at their door, and Emma was no exception.

"Oh, dear," said the host in his faux Lancastrian accent, placing his arm around Emma's shoulders as he forced his way in to her home. "I'm used to making women wet, but not on their face."

Kwyatt put a hand to his mouth, feigning shock, and uttered his catchphrase. "Oooh, what am I like?"

Every inch the creep you appear on the FeedBox, thought Emma.

"Hey, it's okay." The host pulled a handkerchief from his breast pocket and dabbed at her face. "Let's stop those foxy faucets, eh? Honestly, if your mascara runs any faster it'll be begging for sponsorship. Oooh, what am I like?"

The host's entourage streamed in after him, and began putting more cam-drones to flight, fixing lights and erecting the Passing Pod. The pod was to preserve Emma's dignity and spare those dearest to her the trauma of witnessing her final moments. It was designed to sanitise the act and nullify their guilt, but for a small fee discerning viewers could, of course, have full access to the Passing Pod in order to support the subjects on their way. Most people paid.

Drones ransacked Emma's home for the possessions that her son Daniel had already identified as valuable, and then delivered them to her dining table. A crew member positioned the items neatly so that the online audience could better see them. Later, within minutes of Emma's death, they would be auctioned online for the benefit of her family. The better she performed, the greater the emotional connection she'd strike with the audience, and the more money she'd raise.

Her family marvelled at the work going on around them, and Emma was disappointed but not surprised to notice the smug expression staining her son's face. There was something else there, too. *Pride.* He was actually proud of bringing death into her home.

With her family's attention elsewhere, Kwyatt's hand fell to Emma's behind and he gave it a hard squeeze. Emma winced, more from the pressure on her sore back as Kwyatt's arm brushed it, than his unwanted and uninvited attention. Kwyatt quickly put his arm back round Emma's shoulder and she glanced at him. He threw her a wry smile but his cold eyes told Emma that she was his plaything. Kwyatt Dreemz had already been an old man in her youth, when he seemed to be on every entertainment show going. He would be a worthy 'contestant' for his own show were it not for the surgical and digital enhancements that kept him looking permanently thirty-eight. Emma's wrinkles may make her look older than Kwyatt, but at least they were hard won and honestly displayed.

Kwyatt turned Emma towards a hovering camera. Its iris adjusted to the light as if examining her, as if trying to discern the value of her very soul, and with that the butterflies in Emma's stomach took flight.

"Now, then. Emma from New Bolton – *Ooh! What an old-fashioned name!* Welcome to You Can't Take It With You, the show where your selfless sacrifice will give your family the riches you couldn't provide them in life. Now, I'm sure you've seen the show, Emma, and you know why I'm here, but do you know who made all this possible?"

"No," Emma lied, "I've no idea."

The host turned to camera. "It was your loving son, Daniel. He was so worried after your recent fall that he contacted our offices and begged us to surprise you. He knew you wouldn't want to go into a home, so he arranged for you to ease the burden instead, and make a little money for your family on the side. Isn't that right, Daniel?"

"Yep, that's right, Kwyatt. I want to buy a new VisuWall, life subscriptions to the best Streamaz for the whole family, and have enough left over to buy a face transplant for my daughter so she can start her own Feeda channel and become a star."

"But there's nothing wrong with Carabeena's face." Emma blurted, instantly regretting it. The viewers wouldn't like that.

"Well, that's not what the socials say, and who are we to argue with public opinion?" Kwyatt offered the screen on his watch as proof. "I mean, I'm not saying she scares horses, but she's the only eight-year-old I know with a restraining order from Aintree." The same hand to mouth, the same face, the same catchphrase that had worn thin years ago. "Oooh, what am I like?"

Her family's laughter hurt Emma more than Kwyatt's words ever could.

"Now then, Daniel. Let's have a look at the valuables that your mother won't be taking with her."

Daniel passed him a wooden box, which Kwyatt placed on the table and unlocked.

Kwyatt rifled through it greedily until he found what he was looking for. "Oh, now. What's this?" Kwyatt pulled a silver locket from the box and opened it. "If I'm not mistaken this is you with a handsome young gentleman."

"Yes, that's right." said Emma.

"A little birdy's told me that it's your dead husband."

Emma nodded.

"Your one and only true love, cruelly taken from you at far too young an age. We can see from the picture that he's wearing a uniform. I believe he was in the army and fought in the Afghan war at the turn of the century. Is that right?"

Emma nodded again and stared at the locket dolefully, as she was expected to do. *Need to keep the audience happy.*

"I'm sorry to hear that," lamented the host, who cast a grave expression to the nearest camera, "but we mustn't judge. Veterans can be charming and appear all too human at first."

And back to Emma. "So why don't you tell us and the people onfeed what happened to him?"

"He was ambushed on patrol. They fought back, but Kevin had... Kevin had been hit. All over."

She expected some consolation from her son, a gentle touch, a shoulder on which to unleash her anguish, but none came. People took a dim view of veterans now, but she was talking about his father, for goodness sake. She felt something squeeze her hand and looked down to see her granddaughter Carabeena smiling at her.

"He was taken to a field hospital, wasn't he?" asked Kwyatt, "and he had so many holes in him they couldn't patch him up quick enough. They blocked one hole and then blood would just spurt out of somewhere else like something off a cartoon."

Emma suppressed sobs as Kwyatt related the last sentence with all the glee and excitement of a drunkard relating a humorous anecdote.

"Well, we managed to track down one of the nurses who looked after Kevin before he passed away, and do you know what they called him at the hospital? You'll love this, Emma. Colander!"

Kwyatt chuckled to the camera. "Isn't that wonderful, viewers! And I believe the locket's not the only thing of his that you've kept hold of? Apart from his pension, that is! Oooh, what am I like?" Kwyatt donned the glasses that hung round his neck, and adopted a serious expression and tone. "Your son tells me you also have his service pistol."

"Now, antique firearms are very valuable, and it would make a lot of money for your family. Might even raise enough to get your granddaughter's mug fixed."

"I don't know. I got rid of a lot of things after he… "

"Are you sure you don't know? It would really make a difference to your family's fortunes."

Emma shook her head.

Kwyatt looked ever-so-slightly crestfallen. "Well, don't worry because we'll get this locket valued, and the house, and see how much money we can get, because, let's face it," Kwyatt raised his hands, inviting the family to join in, which they duly did. "You can't take it with you!"

Kwyatt Dreemz set off for the table at which the antiques expert – Tarantulo da Pawn – sat expectantly, and beckoned Emma's family to follow him.

Emma didn't move, and instead looked down at the mahogany box, a time-worn but clearly treasured heirloom, from which Kwyatt had stolen the locket. It was her reminiscence box, full of the physical catalysts from which her memories sprang. Emma pawed the photographs within and paused at one of them. It was a photo of her wedding; the two of them so happy, souls united and looking forward to a bright future. They were so young, barely in their 20s. Then another photo caught her eye. It was the two of them with their friends at a chain restaurant. Everyone beaming from ear to ear and radiating happiness as if they were having their best night ever, even though it was probably just another week-night meal. How quickly things had changed.

"Who are those people, Grandma?"

Emma turned to see Carabeena gazing at the photographs with genuine curiosity.

"Oh, these are pictures of my friends, and your grandad."

"Why aren't they moving? Have the batteries run out?"

"Oh, these aren't screens, baby girl. These are photographs. They're just paper."

"You look so happy. They all do."

"We were. We were blessed, and we didn't even know it."

"Who's that?" said Carabeena, pointing to a photo of her grandma and a frail-looking man in an armchair.

"That's John, your great-grandad. My dad."

"Why's he so old? Was he selfish?"

"No, things were different then. Just because you were old, it didn't mean you had to die. Your great-grandad lived until he was eighty-six."

"That's ancient! I don't know of anyone who's lived past sixty."

"Well, that was normal when I was a little girl. Some people were just getting married and settling down at my age."

"So why do they have to ease the burden now?"

Ease the burden. It saddened Emma to hear her granddaughter use that dreadful euphemism.

"Only the very poorly eased the burden in those days. People had terrible illnesses that couldn't be cured. They were in constant pain and couldn't take anymore, so the government let them go peacefully. Your great-aunt Pat did that. She was in a terrible state, and easing the burden gave her peace and stopped her suffering for many more months.

"Then everyone lost their jobs, they got rid of the hospitals that mended people for free, and no-one could afford to look after the elderly and the disabled. People were so desperate to feed themselves that the old and the ill were talked into killing themselves so they didn't make their families any poorer."

Carabeena hugged Emma tight. "I don't want you to die, grandma. I don't want a new face, I'd rather have you. Can't you say no?"

"I can't do that, Carabeena. It's not about what I want; it's about what other people want."

"Will I have to ease the burden when I'm older?"

What a question for an eight-year-old to ask, and what a question to answer. Emma couldn't lie, but she didn't have to tell the truth either. "You won't have to think of that for a very long time, and, when you're older… Well. Things don't have to be the same as they are now. You and your friends can change things when you grow up."

Emma turned to see Kwyatt and her family approaching. Her time was up.

"Well, Emma, we were a little worried there when Tarantulo said we'd only have enough for a digital facelift, but at the last minute someone bid out of nowhere and bought the house for way more than expected." Kwyatt leaned towards Emma conspiratorially. "Do we have an admirer on feed, Emma?"

Emma forced a smile.

"Now then, Emma," said Kwyatt with his trademark false solemnity. "It's time for you to say goodbye to your family and enter the Passing Pod, where you can take the drink and ease your family's burden. Is there anything you'd like to say before you enter?"

"Yes," said Emma. "I want you to watch." She put her hand in the wooden box, clicked a concealed switch and opened a hidden compartment.

Her son and his wife looked puzzled. So did Kwyatt.

"I want you to see what death looks like, Daniel. And everyone else onfeed. I want you to see the consequences of your actions and I want you to live with them for the rest of your days."

Emma pulled a black, metallic object from the compartment with her right hand and clicked the clip in to place with her left. It was her husband's pistol. She knew there were at least five rounds in the magazine. Emma pulled the receiver back to cock the weapon and prayed that the gun still worked.

"I'm afraid that's not how it works, Emma," said Kwyatt. "This is supposed to be a selfless act, a dignified finale that spares your loving family the pain of your passing. That's what you want, isn't it? To go peacefully and free them from the burden of nursing you?"

"Nursing me?" said Emma incredulously. "I'm only fifty-two, I've got years ahead of me yet. I had one fainting spell after a bad dose of flu. I'm hardly an invalid in need of round-the-clock attention and my arse wiping thrice a day."

Carabeena laughed quietly then stopped when Daniel slapped her lightly on the shoulder.

"I'm sorry, Emma." said Kwyatt, dropping his happy man-of-the-people manner and adopting a more authoritative tone. He motioned to the show's medic and then to Emma. The medic reached into his bag, extracted a syringe and then slowly edged towards Emma. The doctor had come across less enthusiastic subjects before and he knew exactly what Kwyatt wanted.

"Sadly, viewers, confusion is common in the elderly," said Kywatt to a hovering cam-drone, "especially if they've had a busy day, like Emma's had today. In those cases we need to calm them down to give them a relaxed, dignified send-off."

"What on earth are you on about, you deluded monster? Death isn't dignified. It isn't selfless and isn't something you can sanitise. This…" Emma gestured towards the cameras, crew and equipment with her free hand. "The way you treat other people, the elderly, the infirm, the disabled, it isn't natural. For God's sake, I'm your mother, Daniel. *How can you do this to me?*"

"Please, Emma!" snapped Kwyatt Dreemz. "Less of the G word. This is a family show."

"Shut up, you twisted, wicked man." Emma trained the gun on Kwyatt, who shrank back a little. "If it's so selfless and dignified why hide us away in a fucking box? Why sneak the body away so no-one sees it?"

Emma pressed the barrel to her temple.

"You know what? Screw it. I want you all to feel the horror, to suffer the nightmares and to be haunted by the reality of my messy death every waking day."

Kwyatt placed a hand to his ear as he listened to a remote voice and looked concerned. He studied the floating monitor and winced as various charts fluctuated on screen.

"Come on, now," pleaded Kwyatt, who seemed genuinely anxious. "A lot of viewers have paid good money to see you pass in the pod. Do you really want Daniel to miss out on all that cash?"

Emma squeezed her eyes shut and felt the tension of the trigger.

"Think about your granddaughter!" shouted Kwyatt. "Look at her, she's terrified. Do you really want her to remember you as the selfish woman who blew her brains out on an international feed just to prove a point?"

Emma uttered her final words calmly. "I do."

Glue Guns in Paradise
Scott Talbot Evans

A call comes over the radio: "Suspect with knife at Liberty Pole. Armed and dangerous."

In the passenger seat, Lieutenant Spoct spits out his dog biscuit. "Holy Schmolies!" He barks deeply, twice.

Lieutenant Liesl Healy punches the accelerator, and the wheelless open-top convertible speeds three feet above the ground. "No one's committing violence on my watch."

The siren, designed to be easy on the ears, sounds like a man singing, "Ooooooo-waaaaaa. Ooooooo-waaaaaa." The German Shepherd plops his front legs over the side and howls in unison.

53-year-old policewoman Liesl cranks hard to the left, then to the right, weaving the mirror-finish chrome sports car between bicycles and pedestrians.

Art: Mark Toner

Spoct's computer eyeball projects a rotating green hologram of a knife onto the windshield. "The blade is 19.4 inches."

She winces at the sight. The thought of what it could do makes her a little queasy. "You could've just said 19 inches. I would've gotten the picture."

"Accuracy is a virtue." He smiles, canine cheeks fluttering in the wind. "It's that last point four inches that gets ya."

"That's not a knife. It's a machete!" Liesl laughs. "Better get the blubber." She presses a button on her belt and an inch-thick clear gel rises over her whole body. Spoct does the same.

Their police hats stay firmly on their heads as the curvy sports car flies 100 mph. "Prevention Force" is written on its sides, in white letters on a blue background. The chassis comes to sharp points at the four corners, poking forward and back, like jousting lances.

Spoct shakes his head. "A knife!"

Liesl's chubby cheeks frown. "What's the world coming to?"

"We should've counseled him the moment he displayed pre-violent behavior." His normally erect ears droop.

"Maybe there wasn't any. Some people just snap." Liesl shakes her head. "Some way to start the new year." Her face expands in excitement and contracts in concentration as she weaves through obstacles, keeping mostly to the right lane, reserved for emergency vehicles and the occasional antique gasoline automobile. Her eyes open wide when a pigeon flies right in front of the car, almost shish kebabing itself. She swooshes past a man pushing a hover cart, causing him to drop boxes and scare a horse-squirrel up a tree. "Sorry," she says, already long gone. She accelerates through a straightaway and shouts with teenage enthusiasm, "I love my job! Woo-hoo!"

"If I could bottle what you're on, I'd be a rich dog."

"You are rich." She beams. "We are abundant!"

Downtown Susan is abuzz. Construction sites on every block. Luxury apartment buildings popping up faster than varmints on a whack-a-mole board. This city is going places—up. Rents are inflating so fast they make an audible whoosh. If you have to ask about parking fees, you can't afford them.

As they approach Liberty Plaza, Liesl says, "Get your gun ready."

His paw taps it. "Don't worry." He peels open a wide doggie grin. "It's always ready."

The plaza is crowded. Little snow mountains are scattered about where the plows scraped them. The Liberty Pole is a two-thousand-foot-tall silver beam circled by wires strung from its apex to the ground. Around the base is a black marble bench where people usually sit, but presently only one man is standing on it, screaming his brains out. The onlookers leave a bubble of space around him on account of the machete he is waving around wildly. The 330-pound man with overgrown hair and dirty clothes is ranting unintelligibly.

The crowd parts for the police car, which skids mid-air to a stop, then gently lowers to the ground.

The man's eyes are out of it. "You people are all cowards! All sheep!"

Healy sees the pain on his face. Her cheeks drop and she feels like crying. She thinks, *How could we have failed someone so badly?* She points the ID pen at him. It identifies his DNA and his complete record comes up: Raymond Michael Franks, Social Security # 581-653-479-291-008, medical, employment, his GoogBook posts going back thirty years. He doesn't like being called Ray. She whispers to Spoct, "Hyponitric psychosis."

Spoct jumps out of the car and calmly approaches to a distance of twenty feet. "How's it going, Ray?"

"Don't Ray me!" He slashes the sword.

Spoct flinches. He cringes at how dirty the man's fingernails are. *This man hasn't washed in 9.2 months.* He presses a button and his body is sealed inside a germ-blocking film. "Take it easy, buddy. We're on your side."

Raymond snarls. "I'm not your buddy." He swoops the blade in the other direction.

Spoct doesn't budge. He holds up one claw to make a point. "Please remember The Four Agreements. Never take anything personally."

Healy approaches within 10 feet. She is 5'7", full figured, with a large pair of chestseses. She takes off her cap, unleashing her wild bush of Ludwig Van Beethoven hair.

Machete Guy grimaces at her. "Screw you and the horse you rode in on!"

The anguish in his eyes, for some reason, brings her back to a dog she knew a long time ago. She would pass it every day on the way to school, and it would bark rabidly. *It wasn't the dog's fault. The owner kept him on a heavy chain, even in freezing weather. Its water bowl was usually turned over in the dirt.* A sickly feeling ferments in the pit of her stomach. She tried befriending the poor animal, but the owner wanted it to be mean. She would talk to it kindly. *I should've called Animal Protection. But I was only fifteen. I didn't know any better.* All these memories flashed through her mind in an instant. She turns to Raymond. "You don't have to be afraid of us, Mr. Franks. We're here to help you."

"The whole government is corrupt!"

Spoct's eyebrows hop, because it's an interesting statement. He takes a step closer. The man's shoes are split open, revealing toes dirty as shoe leather. He stinks of urine. Spocts worries that if he can smell it, some germs must be getting through the barrier.

Healy searches Raymond's face for a trace of humanity.

Spoct stands on his hind legs and spreads his arms. "You can't be out in this snow. At least let us give you some proper shoes."

"I'M NOT TAKING ANY FREAKING MEDICATION!"

"No one said anything about medication. What do you take us for, barbarians?"

Healy chuckles inside because she is one of the few 'lucky' people who still takes medication in the antiquated pill form. She holds her chest. "Please let us help you."

He points the weapon at her.

At least he stopped waving it. That's progress. I must be getting through to him. Nonviolent communication training taught her how to phrase a request. "Would you be willing to put the knife down?"

"I'm not putting anything down until Congress turns themselves in to the authorities."

Spoct and Healy side-eye each other. Not bloody likely.

"Congress kills millions of people. Why don't you arrest them?"

Spoct is now eight feet away. He speaks calmly, "If you have a complaint, we can file a report, but right now you are the one brandishing a dangerous weapon."

Raymond tilts his head, looks at the knife, then back at Spoct as if to say, "By gosh, you're right."

"I hate to be that guy, but I really have to insist you put it down." Spoct shifts his weight in case he has to leap suddenly.

Liesl takes a step closer. "Try taking a slow deep breath. I promise you'll feel better." She demonstrates.

Raymond shows no response, but then takes a long deep breath. He locks eyes with her, and they deep breathe together a few times.

She smiles. "Isn't that better?"

Raymond scratches an itch on his arm.

"Are you okay?"

He scratches faster. Whines as if the itch is getting worse.

"You can try tapping." She takes one hand and gently karate chops the other hand rhythmically.

Spoct analyzes his behavior. He whispers into his radio, "Be careful, Liesl. 31% probability of violent outburst."

She whispers back, "That means 69% chance of nonviolence. Deep down he's just a frightened little boy." She smiles. "Raymond, can I come over and talk?" He seems okay. She comes within five feet. "May I?" She doesn't wait for an answer and sits.

It makes Spoct nervous that she is within leaping distance. He whines and readies his legs.

Raymond looks down and ogles her. It's not clear how he will react. He slowly sits.

Her heart warms. She takes in the sunshine and clean air. "Isn't it a beautiful day?" She reaches in her jacket. "Would you like a nice pair of wool socks. I knitted them myself."

Raymond stares at them, then points his crooked finger. "What are those?"

"Ducks. I knitted them using the intarsia method."

He nods, impressed.

"Would you be willing to put that knife away? It makes me nervous." She was going to say one more thing, but changed her mind, so instead makes a short hum.

Spoct shakes his head at her trusting nature. He locks eyes on the subject, calculating how long it would take for him to swipe at her and coils his muscular hind legs like steel springs.

Raymond softens, takes a breath and says, "Okay." He digs the blade into the snow and smiles. "It makes me nervous too."

It's working. I'm making a connection. She grins at Spoct, who doesn't reduce his vigilance one bit.

A second patrol car pulls up.

Spoct waves at them to stay back. "Healy is handling it."

Liesl hands Raymond the socks. "Would you like to put them on?"

He slowly reaches for them.

Spoct watches for sudden movements.

The newly arrived officers are Hatch, a large athletic man, and Smoob, an eight-foot-tall grizzly bear. Great folks once you know them, but at first sight, wearing protective gear and carrying large bazookas, quite intimidating. Raymond sees them advance and cries in panic. He grabs the machete and chops Healy's neck.

She shudders. The blade bounces off the blubber. In a flash, Spoct punches his 200 pounds into Raymond's chest, knocking him down. They tumble on the ground, and Spoct rolls to his feet with the blade in his teeth.

Raymond gets up and runs screaming toward Healy.

Both hands hold the gun and she fires a line of green goo dead center at his chest. Spoct hikes his leg, spraying a second stream of florescent green glue.

Raymond keeps screaming and charging with clawing fingers.

Liesl steps back, continuously spraying him.

Raymond tries to wave the gunk off his arm, but it sticks. He tries to wipe it off, but when he pulls his hand away, it snaps back.

Hatch and Smoob join in with thick torrents from their supersoakers. Raymond is covered and moving slower as it thickens. It hardens and he turns into a statue.

Hatch takes off his helmet. He is handsome with a large purple afro. He walks up to the prisoner and says, "You shouldn't a oughtn't a done that."

A muffled scream comes from the sarcophagus.

Hatch snaps his fingers. "I can't hear you."

Smoob pokes her claw into the green plastic, opening a hole for the detainee to breathe, releasing his angry rants to the world. She widens it to expose his whole face and smooths it out to pretty her artwork.

"Get your stinking paws off me, pig!"

Smoob has an upper-class Southern accent. "I think someone needs a lesson in basic zoology."

In front of the captive's face, Spoct's eye projects a video about the biological differences between bears and pigs. "I know he was speaking figuratively, but why pass up a teachable moment?" He wags his tail. "I do love teaching so much."

Smoob taps the mound of hardened goop. It makes a pleasing clink. She tips it over with one hand. Hatch catches the other end and they set it down behind their car. They connect the tow cable as he screams, "Death to King Sanders!"

Hatch sighs. "You realize President Sanders has been dead for fifty years?"

Spoct shakes his head. "How could our education system have failed so badly?"

Hatch puts his arm around the statue. "Take it easy, baby. We are going to treat you like a prince."

Raymond quiets down.

Hatch and Smoob climb into their vehicle with their cargo, and it rises three feet.

Smoob turns back to their passenger. "We haven't had any complaints yet, sugar."

They take off.

Liesl and Spoct watch them go.

Spoct notices that the usual smile on Liesl's face is missing. He puts a supportive paw on her arm. "Quite an ordeal."

She sighs.

His paw strokes her arm. "You were physically attacked. You have every right to be shaken up."

"That's not it. What bothers me is that a disturbed guy was roaming the streets and not one officer intervened."

"It doesn't bother you that you were almost decapitated?"

"But I wasn't."

"But I hate to think what could have happened." He hops back in the squad car.

Healy climbs in. "If there's nothing you can do, then don't worry about it."

Spoct stares into the distance. "I wish it were that easy."

They head back to the station. The hole in the crowd fills.

\#

Nestled in snowy, wooded hills is a log-cabin-style luxurious ski chalet. The whole front wall is glass, displaying grand foyer with inviting fireplace to the cold outside world. The sign over the entrance says:

Smoob drives round to the rear and backs up to the loading dock. Hatch watches in the side view mirror. "You're good. You're good."

Robotic conveyors extend, coddle the little green mountain, and draw it in like an automatic car wash. Attendants Ed and Phil, in lab coats, face masks, gloves, and rubber boots, guide it along. It passes through an arch that scans Raymond's physiology. His medical issues are cataloged. None urgent. Plantar fasciitis. Hangnail.

Hatch drops the machete down a chute. The dead metal clinks down a shaft and lands in a furnace, where it is melted down. The liquid runs through a duct into a mold which shapes it. It hardens and drops out the other end as an attractive figurine of President Thunberg. Smoob catches it, still warm, and juggles it to cool it off. She holds it up. There's little Greta, with a big smile on her face and her famous pig tails. "Now isn't that better?" She hands it off to Phil, who places it on a shelf with others, slated for distribution to needy families.

Phil turns on the showers from several angles. The glue dissolves, exposing Raymond curled up on the floor, sleeping like a baby. Dirty water swirls down the drain.

"He really needed a bath," Phil says.

"Bien sur." Ed scrubs him with a long handle broom.

Smoob grabs a sponge, and Hatch a mop, and they wash him.

Meanwhile at the front of the building, Healy and Spoct quickly enter through automatic doors. Spoct runs ahead onto the center of the marble floor, sits, and barks twice. An officer waves hi and says, "Hey, buddy."

Two cops are chatting in the lobby. One says, "Did you hear the news? Someone was brought in for brandishing a knife." The other looks shocked.

Healy marches past the front desk without slowing. The Sergeant behind it says to her, "Room D."

As Raymond sleeps in a leather lounge chair, a nurse cures his kidney disease with an injection and his heart rhythm with a magnetic paddle. Then she rolls him into the beauty salon where Ed and Phil trim and polish his nails. Matted hair and beard are washed, combed, cut, and styled. They massage him, rub in skin lotion, and dress him in plush bathrobe and fur slippers.

They wheel him, still snoring, into a room with medical devices. Healy is there, dressed in a surgical gown.

The captain says to her, "He's all yours."

Healy puts a helmet covered in wires over Raymond's head. She flicks switches, enters numbers, and examines images of neurons and pathways of electric current. Another screen shows chemical interactions and systems-level pathogenesis.

"No signs of epilepsy, bipolar, or dementia," Healy says into a microphone.

The picture shows molecules interacting.

Healy continues to record: "I'm not seeing any depression or OCD. It looks pretty good. Oh wait. I'm detecting high activity in the anterior cavern of Pratt." The laser zooms in on an area behind the ear, which is shaped like a funny walnut. "Isolating." She zooms in further and examines the goings-on inside cell walls. The mitochondria float around like giant jellybean sea creatures. "Increasing magnification by 1000." Inside is a storm of jagged rocks. Molecules containing myriad atoms firing like spark plugs. She examines neurotransmitters. Goes down a chain of carbon atoms until she finds protein DISC1. A group of atoms dancing, bumping and grinding, do-si-doing, trading hydrogens, and combining. "There. See. Polymorphism." It zeroes in on an empty spot where a nitrogen atom should be, which blinks red. "Bingo."

Healy wheels over a large machine and puts the hole around his head. She turns on a panel. A powerful light comes from inside like a nuclear tanning bed. She works a joystick, controlling microscopic tweezers, and delicately places a single nitrogen atom into the vacancy. It snaps in place and spins like home sweet home.

She watches a minute to make sure the genes are replicating themselves correctly, which they are.

"Fresh as a daisy!" She takes the instrument off him and sits him up, presses a button and he wakes. "How are you feeling?"

"Fine. Who are you?"

"I'm Liesl."

"I'm Raymond."

"Do you remember me?"

"Oh yes. You're that nice lady with the duck socks."

She giggles. He looks so different cleaned up and psychosis-free—gentle, intelligent, like a university professor.

He looks around. "Weren't we at the Liberty Pole?"

"We brought you here because you were waving a knife around. Do you remember that?"

"Yes. I do." He is embarrassed. "I'm sorry. I don't know what got into me."

"You were missing a nitrogen atom in your temporal lobe, but don't worry, we got it."

"Thank you." He scratches his head. "How long was I out for?"

Spoct trots in wearing a white coat, stethoscope, and head lamp. "Let's finish your physical exam." He pulls off one of Raymond's slippers with his mouth, steps on it and chews it. Sniffs his foot. "You're lucky you didn't get frostbite. Your toes were blue." Spoct taps his knee with a rubber hammer. "Reflexes normal." He taps his back with his paws. "Your lungs sound good. Turn your head and cough." He looks in his ears with a viewer and passes a scanner over his limbs. "No arterial blockage. Excellent." He peers through another device. "Ooh, look at this. You have a precancerous cell in your pancreas that is going to turn malignant in about seven years."

"I do?"

His paw presses a button. "Nipped it in the bud. Very good. You're as healthy as a horse."

By coincidence, a doctor who happens to be a horse clops by the open door, smiles and nods.

Spoct pats Raymond on the shoulder. "You have the physique of a thirty-year-old."

"I am thirty."

"Then you're right where you should be."

"People tell me I look thirty."

"That's only fair." Spoct goes over to a wall of computer screens and flips through data. "Heart, lungs, everything looks pretty good, but there are a couple of issues we have to deal with. Did you know you have a touch of glaucoma? It's nothing serious, but we'll have to keep an eye on it." He adds a note to the chart. "I see you're short on sleep."

"How do you know that?"

"Your brain chemicals tell the whole story. Don't worry. It's probably just from the psychosis."

"I *am* rather tired."

Spoct holds a tube near his arm, giving him a needle-less injection which makes a spritz sound. "How's that?"

"Wow. I feel fully rested."

"I see you're running on the heavy side. Are you happy with your weight?"

"I've been trying to lose weight my whole life, but I can't seem to do it."

"How much would you like to lose?"

He holds his belly. "I don't know. 150 pounds would be a good start."

Spoct takes an instrument resembling a hand-crank eggbeater and works it near the back of his head. "A little more." He stops. "You're all set. You'll lose two pounds a week until you reach your goal." He turns to Healy. "That's everything on my end."

Healy takes Raymond's arm. "Raymond, why don't we go to my office where we can be a little more comfortable?"

It looks more like someone's den than an office. It has comfy chairs and many personal items, including artworks by Liesl; a painting of a king on a throne, and a knitted albino doll with a cochlear implant. The view out the window is lovely.

She fixes him a hot chocolate.

He sips it. It warms him. He holds the mug tight, like a lifeline, his only possession in the world. He frowns. "Am I going to jail?"

She laughs. "You watch too many old movies. Jails were abolished a long time ago."

"Yeah, but attempted murder of a police officer."

"Oh please. You were obviously suffering from a serious brain disorder. Anyone could see that."

He smiles. "That's a relief."

"No. In fact, the real villain here is the system. I still can't figure out how we failed to detect a person with so many problems for so long."

"I was offered help…many times…but I always refused."

"It's a tricky thing. We can't force anyone."

"I just wanted to be left alone."

"Psychosis is a tough one. Your mind is your own worst enemy. You feel guilt, self-contempt, fear. You can't control anything, and yet everything is your fault."

Raymond nods sadly. "You've described it very well."

"I've had a lot of experience in these matters. You must remember these are all symptoms of a disease. Don't blame any of it on yourself." She pats his hand. "Do you remember talking about President Sanders? You seemed to be very angry at him."

"That was just the psychosis talking."

"You're probably right, but sometimes it indicates an underlying issue."

"Why wouldn't I like him? He was one of our greatest presidents, next to Malala."

Healy raises an eyebrow. "You said he was a Marxist."

"Oh, fiddle faddle. I was out of my mind. I was listening to radio talk shows 24 hours a day. I thought everyone was a Marxist. I thought the Russians were trying to sabotage the Postal Service."

"And now you don't?"

"I used to think that every streetlamp had a surveillance camera."

"So, you don't think that anymore?"

"I still do, but now I understand it's for our own protection."

"I'm going to make a little adjustment." She attaches a probe to his temple. "Now I'm going to show you a picture." A picture transmits through the probe, showing him a black and white publicity photo of a well-known senator sitting in a regal pose. "What do you think when I show you this?"

"He's a Communist!"

"That's what I thought." She dials down the instrument. "How about now?"

"He's a Socialist!"

She reduces it a little more. "And now?"

"He's a neo-libertarian-pseudo-reformed-Socialist."

"Okay. Better. I think we're good. I don't think you'll be experiencing any more hallucinations. We'll monitor you, but my guess is you're going to be fine." She makes some notes. "Do you have a place to stay?"

"Yes, under the bridge on Clinton Avenue."

"The one next to the Veteran's Outreach Center?"

"Exactly."

"Would you like an apartment?"

He almost laughs. "Gee, I don't know. What can I get for zero per month?"

"Don't worry about money. You don't think we would release a distressed person onto the streets without a place to stay?

That would be ridiculous. I'm writing you a voucher for a one-bedroom apartment."

"You're giving me an apartment? How long can I stay there?"

"As long as you like."

He looks at her with suspicion. "Who's going to pay for it?"

"It's on us."

"How can you afford to do that?"

"How could we afford not to? If we allowed you to be homeless, it would only end up costing us more in social services."

"Thank you so much. I'm sorry about the whole knife thing." He makes a swiping gesture.

Liesl places her hand on top of his. "I'm the one who should be apologizing to you. It was my job to prevent this from happening. We should have picked up the warning signs a lot sooner." She diligently wiggles her fingers a foot away from the screen, entering notes. "Don't worry. I'm going figure out where we went wrong." She hands him a slip of paper. "Just go to this address and the building manager will give you your keys."

"When I'm on my feet, I'll pay back every penny."

"Not necessary. It's covered by insurance." She hands him an informational pamphlet titled, *Relax. You have a Rich Uncle.*

"I don't know what to say." He cries from happiness.

They hug.

The Alien Invasion

Ely Percy

Ah wis abducted by aliens wance. Never tolt anywan but. It wis nearly forty year ago an ah knew whit folk wid say. The wans in ma class wid be aw, Did yi aye? Zat when yi had yir first anal probe? Zat why yir a fuckin space cadet? Probly widda thought ah wis jist makin it up fur attention anyway. Ma ma an da definitely wid. That's whit they tried tae say that time ah smacked ma heid aff the livin room waw after ma da shoved me oot the road ae the telly – they tried tae say thir wis nothin up wi me, that ah wis jist pure at it, pure tryin tae get extra time aff school.

Fair play, ah did huv previous – ah'd a bit ae bother aff Mister Bueller the Maths teacher cause ah twice got caught doggin his tutorials. Yi'd still hink sumdy widda took me tae the hospital though. Ah tolt them umpteen times ah wis feelin weird, an ah'd

Art: Mark Toner

a massive big bruise on the side ae ma noggin. But naw. Ma ma wis like, Och yi'll be fine wance yi huv an early night. Ma da wis jist pit oot cause he knew he'd huv tae forego watchin the rest ae his Channel Four darts tournament. Aye that wull be right, he roart, Ah'm no traipsin aw the way tae the Southern General fur you ya meladramatic wee shite.

No that ma da ever did anythin tae strain hissel. He'd never worked since he left the John Neilson, an his greatest claim as a faither wis the story ae how he used tae take us tae this Buck Rogers restaurant in Glasgow when ah wis a wean. Yi wantet tae see the inside ae this gaff, he'd say whenever he'd an audience, It wis aw done up lik a space-ship – pure brilliant so it wis – an the fid wis served by actual robots an the real waitresses wur dressed as aliens! Accordin tae ma da, ah pure loved it an ah gret the face aff him tae go anytime we wur up the toon. Ah don't remember any ae this by the way; whit ah dae remember is gettin took tae some clatty burger place where the flairs wur aw sticky an thir wis hardly any light; ah got papped in front ae a big projector screen that played reruns ae the same shitey TV show, week in week oot, whilst he got pished wi his pals at the bar.

When ma parents finally phoned an ambulance fur us, it wis a full two days later, an only because ah took a mad seizure whilst helpin ma ma prepare the totties fur wur Sunday dinner. It wis horrible tae see, she said, Yi wur on the flair jerkin away good style still haudin ontae the peeler an yi endet up gougin a big skliff a skin aff yir ain chin. Aye horrible, mumbult ma da, who'd missed the full drama because he'd been watchin V: The Final Battle.

Ma da used tae be heavy intae aw the auld sci-fi programmes – Star Trek, Mork An Mindy, Dr Who, you-name-it; V wis his favourite though, an he'd aw the episodes on Betamax; he also had a signed photie ae Jane Badler aka Diana the evil Visitor that wis his pure pride an joy. After ah hud ma heid injury he startet askin me tae sit an watch his programmes wi him. Ah wisnae really interestet especially since ah'd a constant heidache an ah couldnae concentrate on anythin fur mair than a few seconds, but ah didnae want tae upset him so ah jist did it. Ah knew he felt bad aboot whit he'd done tae me – the doctors said ah'd a fracturt skull an it'd take six months tae heal, but luckily they didnae hink ah'd need invasive surgery; they also said ah'd probly always be left wi slight brain damage. Ma da didnae actually apologise as such, but he chucked the bevvy awthegether, an never wance did he lift his haun tae me again.

Yir probly wonderin by noo whit this has got tae dae wi an alien abduction. Ah like tae hink that everyhin happens fur a reason, an the only reason it happent tae me wis because ah wis doggin school the day the aliens appeart.

Ah'd been sent tae see an educational psychologist yi see. Cannae mind when exactly… a month later… two months… possibly mair… The doctors said ah wis sufferin fae baith post-traumatic an anterograde amnesia as well as other hings. Magine huvin two amnesias? Fuckin nae luck ataw, eh? Anyway, this psychologist come intae the school – she wis wan nosey bastart, pure askin a mullion questions aboot how did ah find ma school work, an how wis ah gettin on wi ma teachers an the other wans in ma class. Noo, ah might no be Brain A Britain but am no *that* stupit – ah knew if ah said anythin aboot the wans in ma class that laughed an slapped thir hauns at me, or the teachin staff who looked the other way, ma life widnae be worth livin. So, ah tolt her everyhin wis fine; ah tolt her ah forgot stuff sometimes, an ah gied her a few examples ae me bein a pure idiot, an she seemed quite happy at that. Then on the mornin ae that second psychology appointment, ah did whit ah always used tae dae whenever ah didnae want tae go tae school – ah kiddet on ah wisnae well – then ah waitet tae ma ma went oot tae her cleanin job, an ma da went doon the bookies, an ah snuck oot tae the Robbie Park.

See tae be honest, ah cannae mind much else aboot that day. Ah wis feelin a wee bit wabbit, an it'd startet tae piss a rain; an wan minute ah wis at the Animals' Corner feedin bits a plain breid tae Sally the goat, an the next thir wis a mad flyin saucer birlin above ma heid.

Yi'd hink sumdy else widda seen a spaceship alightin on the roof ae the hen hoose. Apparently no though. It wisnae whit yi'd caw a subtle entrance either, whit wi aw the squawkin an the shriekin. Tae be fair, it wisnae a very big spaceship – aboot the size ae wur livin room – an it wis a right dreich mornin, an thir wurnae much folk oot an aboot. But still.

Ah'd this sudden blindin heidache right as ah wis lookin up at the thing, followed by another wan ae they stupit fits. When ah woke up ah wis lyin on a gurney an wearin whit looked lik a metal colander roon the tap ae ma heid.

Noo, ah know whit yir probly hinkin. Yir hinkin, Brain injury equals fuckin doolally. Aye, mibby yir right. Mibby ah'm are an extra-special-terrestrial, a weirdo, a queerie lik aw the cunts fae school kept sayin. An mibby ah don't know every single detail ae whit happent tae me that day. But ah'm wan hunner percent positive they wur real aliens ah saw, an that they aliens saved ma life.

Ah felt much better after the aliens unclamped the mad colander fae ma napper an beamed me back doon tae street level. Ah still couldnae concentrate great an ma memory wis the same swiss cheese – but the dizziness, an the nausea, an the constant poundin ah'd hud in the back ae ma skull fur months wis totally gone.

When ma da come oot the bookies he fun me sittin on a waw roon the back ae the Renfra toon hall: ah'd a bottle ae Strike Cola, three big pickles, an a bag a chips fae Dominic's; ah also hud nae clue how ah'd got there or whit'd enabled me tae pay fur a chippy.

No long after that, ah went fur a folly-up the hospital. That wis when aw the palaver ensued between the different doctors, because they couldnae find any trace ae a skull fracture wi thir machines. They did two mair CT scans plus an MRI but still thir wis nada. In the end they decidet that thir hud obviously been a mix-up wi the first x-ray, an that thir wis never any damage tae ma heid ataw.

Ah did hink aboot tellin the doctors that ah'd been abducted by aliens. But ah knew it'd be a big mistake. Ah could jist imagine masel bein wheeched aff tae some random laboratory fur further tests; probly some snide wee orderly wid tell the papers an ma full family wid end up wi the News Ae The World up wur backs.

So ah kept it buttoned an got on wi ma life.

Ma memory never got any better, an school remained shite, but ah learnt tae live wi the deficits, an the educational psychologist – who turnt oot tae be quite nice – continued tae request me every Monday mornin fur the rest ae the year which got me ootae Tutorial Maths. Hings at hame wur much the same: ma ma wis still ma ma, an she still never listent tae a word ah said; an ma da wis still a bit ae a dick, but him an me got on a lot better.

An thir wis wan other good hing that came oot ae aw this – ah realised ah actually quite liked ma da's alien invasion programs.

Ely Percy is the author of a memoir (*Cracked*, 2002) and two novels (*Vicky Romeo Plus Joolz*, 2019, and *Duck Feet*, 2021). More recently, they won the John Le Carre scholarship with their novel-in-progress (*Kingstreet*). They live in Edinburgh.
Ely Percy is a neurodivergent, amnesiac brain injury survivor.

How Yer Glaikit Gran Beat Back The Beat

Callum Dougan

See in Graveside? Two things killed folk. Thae things were the drink and the Beat: I didnae drink. As for the Beat? My stolen steel toes tip-tappin – they aw felt it, the entire bar. Vibrations flowin through the floor, countin four-four? That's how it starts. Once it spreads ye're doomed tae repeat, like Jimmy Hauns the week afore. He tapped oot efter a day's worth, died with forty fingers wedged in dents they'd drummed in the toon lamppost. People said *Well. That's what ye get. Robbin the Graves and ye dare greet? Easy come, easy go.*

Mark stepped back, cleanin a glass. He frowned at the bloody cheek of me. 'Away wi ye.' In aw fairness? The *Bonehoose* didnae need mair Beat, judgin by the crumblin ceilin. Mark was auld and he kent the Beat: how folk caught it and how that'd go and why we went doon there still. So he jist shrugged. 'Take the bottle. But ye're scarin the patrons see.' Easy come, easy go.

'So ye're sayin,' I summarised, ' "oot afore the Beat drops" of course?' I had naewhere – other than there – tae sit waitin for the facin. But his fingers tapped staccato. And he was giein me the Look. The one that said *I cannae afford tae fix the windaes again*. I jist stood there, countin oot time. My heartbeat whispered in Auld Morse: *easy come, easy go*.

Fightin was oot. Everyone tried, and everyone endit up beat. So I figured: jist embrace it. What was the worst that could happen? They wantit me tae go die quiet? Like fu- darn would I die quiet. I'd gie them the deepest damntit drop and one hell of a show. The bottle clinked, full and too low. Poured hauf oot and made my retreat: *easy come, easy go*.

El said 'that's close enough.' I was ten feet away. She was at her windae with her big crossbow. I'd only needed scrap – naebody was lackin, not here in Graveside or anywhere bloody else. But by now the Beat was straight-up beyond hidin. My arms twitched *one-and-two-and-three-and-four-and*. They were gettin faster and faster and wait where was I oh aye El was tellin me tae go die- She looked me in the eye. 'Don't tap out like a fool. Beat only ends one way and it's one you well know: *easy come, easy go*.'

What should I have done ai? Stuck tae bloody hoppin? The deid's parts were poison but we went even so. There's a clue there weanling, a thread one day ye'll pull: how come the poison and how come we'd no forgo? How come the whole Graveside and how come aw the Graves? How come we got the Beat and how come in that place? How come everyone would jist look at ye with a stopped watch face and how come naebody dared riot? Folks wantit me quiet. But I'd gie them a show: I'd show them aw the soul in my new steel big toe: *life's easy come, life's easy go*.

Youse ever tried buildin a stage? When you're deep intae heavy Beat? And the whole toon's wantin somebody else tae take ye aff the street? I wisnae even infectious – unless some eejit stole my parts. Beat was in them aw now frae my tappin feet tae my revvin heart. In hands hammerin with syncopation and thae deep auld deid blues. In my gyroscope spinnin like a young boxer thirteen pints doon. In the hammerstrike and heartbeat and the clock of the Awmighty aw syncin up intae a chorusin wall of slick-thick tune. I couldnae let it drop too soon. There's a right time tae let it go. But the Beat didnae agree and in my soul I heard it echo: *life's easy come, life's easy go-*

But it was comin oan fiercely. So I was runnin oot of time. And I was daein that thing I dae where I cannae help but rhyme. Everything had tae be jist right. I ran a finger doon the line. Every bottle chimin tae an absolute purestrain perfection, every part of me rippin on past aw the factory settins – if they even had them afore the war and the Graves and the Beat – chimin glass and bangin steel for the evergrowin crowd of folk (brave enough tae stay and watch me and cowards enough tae stay back, like I was chock-fullae nitro). The Beat pushin me still louder, my vocaliser tearin up eighty decibels past zero: '*life's easy come, life's easy go—*'

And then I gave myself over. Jist let the Beat in and hit it. Hit it hard as I could afore it tapped me oot for ever, the steel boards whup-whup-whup-wobblin, the drop comin ever closer: I hit it and hit it and hit it but the drop jist didnae come – *impossible* they were thinkin, *nae chance she keeps this up for long* – but like hell was I done yet because I hadnae finished this song (aw I had tae dae was *go on*)-

So that's how I beat back the Beat frae the Graves deep doon deid Glasgow, and by now wean ye've heard me tell it in every key and tempo: *life's easy come, life's easy go—*

Callum Dougan grew up on parts of the internet the news never warned you about. He was an archaeologist once but that career's in ruins. He lives in Edinburgh. You can follow him on Twitter @CallumMDougan .

Relay

Louise Hughes

Relay 41 to Paige: Are you awake yet?

I woke up light-headed and light-bodied, drifting in my cabin with the carpet tiles and the rest of the station above my head. No one else breathed within a billion kilometres. Noa had been gone for twenty-three days.

Me: *I'm awake.*

I tapped the words into the air above my left wrist. Then I dialled up the gravity a bit and re-discovered the floor. I'd been running a challenge last night with Sadie (Relay 48). Repairs in low-g in the event of system failure. The lights were still set to evening, a dull candle glow instead of the bright white of morning. I must have overridden them.

Me to Relay 164: *Good morning. Remember to hydrate.*

I reached for my flask as I sent the message.

Relay 164: *Good morning.*

We weren't close. I rarely saw them on the feed but they were my assigned morning contact today, just like I was Relay 41's. Sole working regulations stipulate regular check-ins with another human, except during sleep hours, and around half of the Deep Space Relay and Distribution Stations in the network are solo staffed. The rest have two operators. It takes a particular kind of person to want to live and work so far out from anywhere.

I completed my checks before breakfast. I like to eat without the paperwork hanging over me. Everything was tight, everything was working correctly, and I had the day's list. It was just another day in the floating warehouse that I called home.

Kevan (Relay 41): *Asa, did you find those seeds?*

Asa (Relay 43): *Yes, the bot misfiled them. They're ready for pick-up.*

Kevan: *I can't believe they got their hothouses up and running so quickly. I thought they'd be on food crates for a few months yet.*

Asa: *Jealous? You know I only deal with the best and brightest.*

Me: *Settler groups are randomly assigned*

Asa: *That's what you think.*

Kevan had had three new settler groups through Relay 41 this month – two to join other groups on already settled worlds in his jurisdiction and one to a new moon.

Porridge bowl in hand, I started down the loading hall that ran almost the full circumference of the station's lowest, storage level. I'd made a cup of tea first thing but damned if I knew where I'd put it, and it wasn't 0900 yet. We run on twenty-four-hour days, all across the Relay Sphere. It ensures continuity for the freight pilots, and the paperwork. We all like continuity out here in the deep.

"Sap?"

"Working."

"Whereabouts?"

"Store B."

I took my porridge to the store and sat outside the door, watching the stars through the wide hall window. Sap came drifting out just as I remembered where I'd left my tea – by the transmitter station in the second level, when I was sending the check-in signals to the settlements. I'd had to wait. The Cascade Group – ten families, they'd been out here four years now – had been late with their return signal. They'd turned the job over to Tom Cascade, the newly minted teen. Something about responsibility.

Sap hovered in front of the window, status light blinking in that considering way. "I finished preparing the stock for Yen Group. We can send a request today, if you want."

I like to be a week ahead with stock, as the big freight ships move so slowly. I also have my doubts about the efficiency of the Earth system warehouses, based on the packing of the freight ships' holds. Noa assured me it was done by algorithm every time I complained.

My settler groups know to have their orders in early.

"We haven't had any new settler groups at all this month."

"Checking."

Sap's access to the band was faster than mine. I had to deal with the UI but they went direct. Machines deal quickly with machines. I'm only really here in case anything breaks, and because the Settler Council back home knows the settlers like a human proxy. When they show up, they talk to me and not to Sap. They talk about books and shows and feeds and art, all of which Sap likes as well. They talk endlessly, like they've just shown up from a silent religious order.

They say it's lonely out here in the dark.

"There are three pending groups. Two Council sponsored. One self-funded. Assignment deadline in ten days."

"I suppose. What if they're waiting for Noa's replacement to get here first?"

Sap didn't answer that. They're efficient, like I like to be, but better at it. They don't waste power on telling me the same thing twice. No one was replacing Noa unless my psych approves it. Noa might never be replaced.

"Marin Group have their assessment and check-ups in four days."

"The calendar's clear?"

"I contacted Relay 41 and 43 to ensure re-routing of transmission traffic."

I wouldn't be able to get onto the feeds until the evaluations were done. All our bandwidth would be needed to relay their calls to the Settler Council psych office. I tapped a reminder into the system, so I had enough reading material. It would affect the downloads as well.

"I'll request system checks on the buoys between here and Earth."

If everything was working properly, they'd be finished faster and I could reclaim my system. As long as there weren't any issues that Marin Group had forgotten to advance file. Some settler groups like to leave everything until the quarterly and it's not as efficient a way of doing things as they think. It clogs up my system and means I can't do things when I normally do them.

Sap stays out of my way on evaluation days. Sometimes I throw things.

"Incoming." The alert system pinged us both. I'd switched off all the annoying flashing lights and sirens.

Neither of us moved. We weren't expecting anyone. I checked the schedule again, because I hadn't finished my cup of tea and that can lead to mistakes. No. Our freight delivery wasn't due for two days and the last one had gone far enough past our area that it would be closer to an outlying border-post than us. I don't really talk to border posts. They're on orbiting planets and continually moving. The ones assigned to my route change all the time.

Me: *Unexpected incoming.*

I pinged the feed and received a series of one word and gesture icon responses back.

Asa: *Have you run a scan?*

Me: *Will do.*

Normally, I wouldn't have bothered them with it. We do get people showing up randomly. Settlers who forget to ping ahead, because they don't understand why it's important. I need to be ready, and how hard is it really to send a quick update? Then I can have the required repair bots and parts ready for their arrival. But no, they treat everything like they're living on a wild frontier.

Anyway, I was on monitoring. Because of Noa. Everywhere was quieter than it should be.

I moved to the nearest access station and ran the scans. The system confirmed the approach of a Type-C vessel – the kind used to ferry supplies, but generally not large numbers of people. They hadn't filed an incoming request so I got the system to ping them a reminder. It's not uncommon, like I said.

Sap ran a calculation while I was doing that.

"They're coming in from the starboard side, sixty-five degrees vertical."

There were four settler groups in that direction, assuming they'd flown straight and not stopped off anywhere. I pulled up a chart for confirmation.

Asa: *Is everything okay?*

Me: *They still haven't filed a request.*

Kevan: *Their transmitter might be damaged.*

Switch to manual. The system checked for a Morse signal first, while transmitting a repeated pattern on the two outboard lights. We also sent a request to the ship's system to allow us to access their internal telemetry, to see what we were dealing with as far as repairs went.

Nothing.

Me: *They're not even transmitting light signals.*

I needed to be in the centre. The access terminals in the landing hall are fine, but they don't have the same resources. Their UI is terrible.

Me: *Are you busy there?*

Asa: *I'm expecting freight this afternoon.*

Kevan: *Just paperwork for me.*

Me: *Can you boost me?*

Kevan: *I'll do it.*

A brief outline of the situation began its journey around the Relay Sphere. It's quicker to send a signal one-by-one than attempt to transmit to everyone at the same time, particularly those on the opposite side of the central Earth system.

By the time I got the ping back around from Asa on the other side, I was in the centre. The consoles there were familiar. I moved across them faster. Especially since Sap had moved Noa's chair out of the way and into Overflow Storage.

"Sap, can you stay by the docking port?"

I'd left them locking down the stores, as we did whenever anyone approached. Standard procedure. It's on the rules pinned to the centre wall. Some people choose to greet docking ships personally but I don't unless there's a problem. Sometimes, I stay up here in the centre the entire time they're here.

Everything is automated. But the system flashed up an error.

No request received.

Whether because of damage or laziness, they hadn't transmitted their docking code. Without it, the system wouldn't let them dock.

Don't imagine this is unusual behaviour. People forget all the time. Other people. People not me. The way I work, I run through the same process every time in the same order, so I can't forget. They approach life haphazardly. Noa used to be a bit like that. Things had become a lot more efficient on my Relay in the last three weeks.

I tried another reminding ping and got nowhere.

I've found that a lot of people swipe away reminders automatically. You can remind them four, five times, and they'll deny ever receiving it.

By then, I had the cameras on my screens. I'm the only one with access to them, and they're one of the reasons I'm here. I can study an image and work out things Sap can't, and the system can't. I can decide, based on what I see, whether to override automation.

I overrode it. The ship was from Marin Group, according to the markings, so they were coming up on their eval. Marin Group had checked in as usual that morning but there had been no messages to tell me about the ship. Marin Group were medium efficiency settlers, with too much spontaneity for my liking. They did things like decide to throw a pasta festival and then complain I didn't have the flour supplies already.

I would be staying up here in the centre until they went away.

As the ship slowed towards the docking port, a cable snaked out to greet them. I had instructed the system to prioritise it so we could communicate over a hard connection before I opened the gate. I do not let anyone through the gate until we've debriefed. They tend to wander about. They try to help with things that are automated and complain when I remind them, because they're "just trying to help".

The line between help and getting in the way is very, very, thin.

Asa: *Status?*

Me: *Attempting to communicate via a hard connection. The ship is from Marin Group.*

The information was added to the boost cycle.

"Relay Station to Marin C Ship, over."

"This is Marin Ship. We're having trouble with our transmitter, over"

"Please send repair request and manifest, over."

"Acknowledged. Relay out."

There was something off with the manifest. It had all the information but in slightly the wrong order. The repair details were also sketchy and I re-read them a couple of times.

"Marin Ship here. Can you open the gate?"

Over. Impatience. You'd think people who'd travelled three days to get here could wait three more minutes.

You'd be wrong.

Something wasn't right, which it never is. I held back on opening the gate and re-read the manifest again. They were requesting dock for transmitter repair, but that couldn't be the reason they were here. They weren't due to be here. They had a store collection next week, on the same day as Yen Group and Over Group.

I like to get my store collections done on fewer days, to minimise disruption.

No one was due today.

I realised that was the point, at the same moment the system alarms started flashing. Unauthorised access in progress. The system tried to hold them out and I kept my hands off so it could concentrate fully on that.

"Someone is trying to break through the gate," Sap said helpfully.

Me: *Someone is trying to break in.*

Kevan: *Transmitting. I'll try and get someone on the border to contact Marin.*

Me: *They checked-in as usual this morning.*

Asa: *Are you okay?*

Me (vocal): "I'm going into the refuge."

I didn't have time to type my response because the refuge door was triple-locked and that took both hands. It's concealed as a floor tile and I open it once every week. On Mondays. I've never had to use it but I need to know I can and do it quickly. I need to know I won't forget the password. Noa used to say I'd remember the sequence if I needed to, but Noa said a lot of things on which we disagreed.

It took two months before she stopped trying to time her breakfast with mine. She was one of those people who sought out others. A rarity in the Relay Sphere but not unknown – she liked meeting the settlers coming and going, and she requested a colleague. I requested no such thing, but six month's in-situ training is mandatory if you've never left planetside before.

The refuge door slid shut above me. The locations vary by station. They wouldn't be able to find me. Inside the small room I had a limited connection to the system, re-routed through many junctions so they couldn't trace it. There was also a kettle and a small crate of food bars. Noa did the last stock rotation and there were all my favourite flavours.

Kevan: *Are you in?*

Me: *I'm in.*

I pulled up the cameras, but I had to cycle through them one at a time now. The screen in was barely thirty centimetres across and the response time was sluggish. The system threw up blocks as the intruders tried to open the gate.

Sap. I couldn't see Sap. They'd been by the gate. I started cycling through the cameras faster, cursing with each lag. It was like working remotely, on a system on another station, thousands of light-years away, inside a molten moon.

Me: *I can't find Sap.*

Asa: *Are they hiding. They might be hiding.*

Another image flashed in front of me. The storage doors, which Sap had locked. Two figures. That was really all there should be on a Type-C ship, but there was another standing by the gate. They'd all put on coats and pulled up the hoods, so I couldn't see them. It made no difference. The system scanned them, identified them by their chips and pulled up ID cards. I swiped the cards off around the Sphere.

Ute, Paulo, and Matt Marin. They were in their late-teens; brother, sister and a cousin. Matt Marin had shipped through six months ago when he finished at university. I'd let the system process him and he'd stayed in his room until the Type-B came to pick him up.

Me: *They're trying to break into the stores.*

Kevan: *You locked it?*

Me: *I locked it. They can't take the supplies.*

Asa: *Stay put, Paige. Stay where you are.*

Me: *They don't know the system. They'll mess everything up.*

A flash, inside my head. I reached up for the refuge door.

Asa: *Stay put.*

She couldn't see me but I stuck my middle finger up at the stream of text over my wrist and slumped back onto the cushion.

Me: *If I go, I can show them where everything is. They won't break anything.*

Asa: *No.*

Kevan: *What does procedure say?*

I didn't reply. Procedure told me to stay in the refuge unless there was a danger to life. I flipped through the cameras again. They were trying to force the door manually. It crept open and I swiped past. The one by the gate had moved off. Paulo. He was thinner than the other two and had a long stride. He was on the stairs, already past the centre level and halfway to the next. The living quarters.

I threw up more locks in a surge of panic.

My space. Keep out of my space. Out of the empty space that had been Noa's, with her fairy lights and incense sticks and posters of waterfalls. An empty space that echoed. Sap had locked the door after a week and refused to give me the code.

Asa: *Paige, what's happening?*

Me: *They're wandering about. They're going near the living quarters.*

Asa: *Have you found Sap?*

I said no but didn't send it, because I found them. The camera images flashed past as I hammered my finger on the keypad, so when I saw them, I had to flick back. No, no, no. Paulo had found Sap. If I hadn't locked so many doors, the support bot might have found somewhere to hide. Sap made a last skid down a hallway towards the locked-off living quarters before Paulo shot a cable from a tech gun and froze them in their tracks.

Support bots are separate from the system and separate from me. I can't access Sap's systems from the refuge, which would be an unfair thing to do anyway.

Me: *They've got Sap.*

Typing it made my shoulders quiver.

I switched on the sound.

"...is the station's operator?" Paulo asked.

Sap didn't reply.

Asa: *Stay put, Paige.*

Me: *They've got Sap. They're in the stores. They're moving everything. They don't understand how it works.*

It would be quicker if I just went down there and showed them. Ute tossed a crate aside and I flinched.

Ilia (Relay 45): *Paige, what would Noa have done?*

I pulled a face at the text. Noa would probably have gone out there.

Paulo had a metal bar. I hadn't seen it before, carried loose on the opposite side to the camera. He raised it and I flicked away.

Ilia: *How did the low-g exercise go?*

Me: *Sadie won.*

Ilia: *How do you think you can improve on that?*

Me: *I should probably practise more. I keep putting it off. Noa used to remind me.*

Noa thought it was her job to do that, because she was the most experienced and I'd started as her trainee.

Sap.

I reached for the keypad.

Kevan: *I've got Jesh Group here. They're the closest to Marin Group. They'd been looped in on the boost.*

Me: *I can't get through to Marin. Something's wrong with their transmitter.*

It wasn't at my end. I could still get through to everyone else. Comms are the most secure part of a relay station.

Kevan: *Jesh have a trader on Marin right now. There was an abundant tomato harvest.*

Asa: *Jesh need tomatoes?*

Kevan: *They've never been good with warm weather produce. They settled too far north and their world orbits, like, at a snail's pace.*

I knew what they'd say back at Settler Recruitment. Although it's technically fine for someone to operate a relay station solo, your psych eval shows that you benefit from company. It's just a matter of...

Asa: *Paige? Are you still there.*

Me: *I'm here. They're trying to find me.*

I could knock out the systems, perform a reset and catch them while the reboot was in progress. I could suck all the air from the dock. I could...

Asa: *They won't. You know that.*

I found a basic game on the wrist system and started moving little blue crates around. It didn't work. I couldn't concentrate and it wound me up tighter. Even without the cameras I knew they were out there, so I flicked them back on. Seeing what they were actually doing was more calming than my imagination. Paulo was hauling Sap back to the dock and I couldn't tell if he'd managed anything other than to immobilise them.

Kevan: *I've got the Marin Group leader here, via Jesh. They want to talk to you.*

Me: *Well, I don't want to talk to them.*

They were out there, destroying my system and causing general havoc. I'd deny their stock requests forever for this. Marin Group could starve.

Asa: *Yes, you do.*

Me: *I really don't.*

Ilia: *Ok, you don't. But we're not talking to them for you.*

Me: *Vocal?*

Kevan: *You can text if you like. Routing.*

I gripped the edges of my chair.

"Hello? Is that the Relay Station?" I hadn't ever spoken to the Marin Group leader. We communicated via paperwork and basic signals and they'd been out there ten years longer than I'd been in deep space.

Me: *Yes. Relay Station acknowledged. Over.*

"I would like to apologise for what has taken place today. We found the ship missing yesterday and did a roll call. We knew they were missing but we never imagined they would do this."

Me: *You checked in as usual this morning.*

"We did not. I imagine they've been intercepting the check-ins. Ute works in communications. Please, route me through to them. They're my siblings' children."

Me: *Why are they doing this? Those supplies are for the other Groups.*

We share equally in Deep Space. To each, according to their need, in a slightly more complicated version of the Basic Survival Allocation on Earth. Freight ships can only carry so much and travel so fast. Once a settler group reaches a certain level of sustainability, they can start putting back in, but so few have reached that yet.

"We don't know. It is unconscionable behaviour. Those supplies will not be welcome back here."

Me: *What about them?*

"They will not be welcomed gladly. Please, let me speak to them."

I had the system do it and while it did, while I let her wait, I reached out again.

Me: *Why would someone take supplies from other settlers?*

Asa: *I don't know.*

Kevan: *It's been fifteen years since anyone tried. I couldn't comprehend it then and I don't now.*

No one else replied. We pondered the impossible question in silence. Those supplies belonged to all of us. They weren't anyone's to take. It just...wasn't the rules. Not rules written on the wall in the centre. The Rules.

"This is Ren Marin. What the hell do you think you're doing?" The Marin leader boomed from the walls of the dock and I routed the comms so the intruders could talk back. Assuming it wasn't a rhetorical question.

"We're taking what's ours," said Paolo Marin. Matt didn't look up from the crate he was carrying. Ute glared at Sap like it was the bot talking.

"Nothing there is yours unless you've requested it."

Matt put the crate down at the gate. "We need these supplies."

"No more than anyone else."

"We never get our fair share. Operator favouritism."

I snapped. What an accusation! "You do. You lying—"

Ren interrupted me. "We get our fair share. If you bring any of those supplies back here, you won't be permitted to land. You can live on them. Don't expect anyone to help you."

"We did this for Marin."

"And Marin tells you, you are doing wrong."

Me: *They said I don't send the supplies out fairly.*

It's the sort of thing incredulous, selfish-minded people say on Earth, about people who decide they'd rather live alone in Deep Space and help people efficiently. Mutterings. There's always mutterings. Noa said that's why she liked to meet the settlers when they came through. Dispel the mutterings.

If I met them, the mutterings would be dispelled with all the efficiency of a megaphone. I know that, however much Noa smiled and said it wasn't true.

Ilia: *We know you do. Everyone knows you do.*

Ada: *You look after your settler groups. We all do. Don't listen to them.*

"This is Grape Jesh, the trade ambassador to Marin Group. We cannot trade with those who steal from us. Think before you do."

I watched on the camera. Sap slid in from the side, picked up the crate Paolo had put down and started back to the store with it. Ute moved aside but Matt lunched forward. He tried to topple the crate.

"That's ours," he shouted.

"It isn't," I said. I wanted them to leave Sap alone to do his job. "I will have Sap load the supplies your group requested in your next shipment. If you go away, I won't report you."

They sulked in a huddle for a moment.

If I reported Marin Group to the Settler Council like I was supposed to, there'd be an inquiry. Everywhere. Of everyone. Maybe even recalls. Very few people were out here because they liked living on Earth.

"We'll take the supplies," said Ute. I think she was in charge.

"Sap," I said. "Please ensure they have the supplies they requested, allowing for fuel allocation."

Type-Cs are designed to fly two passengers and freight, not three. They would need to take some air canisters. I routed the comms back to the refuge.

"This is Ren Marin. I would like to apologise again. I will put in a request for evals as soon as you confirm they've left the Relay. They've been watching shows their cousin brought back. Old shows. The birth-rate is up here and it's been a challenging few years. They thought they were being heroes. We didn't realise it was this serious, and I'm sorry. I should have put in a request earlier. Please don't think Marin doesn't take our settlers' wellbeing seriously."

I didn't know how to respond to that.

Me: *Confirmed. Relay out.*

On the camera, Sap continued to ferry crates, taking their time.

Me: *I think Sap's making them wait on purpose. This will take ages.*

Kevan: *I'd make them wait if I was them.*

Asa: *Are you still in the refuge, Paige?*

Me: *Yes. Can I leave yet?*

Asa: *Stay there until they're gone, I think.*

Kevan: *Better for everyone.*

Me: *Fine.*

I kept the camera on so I could glare at them. That wouldn't do anyone any harm.

Asa: *I've got to go and do some checks. Have you got something you can be getting on with?*

Me: *No.*

Asa: *Nothing?*

Me: *I did the paperwork. I can't do anything else in here.*

Asa: *There must be something. Maybe something you've been putting off.*

She signed off. She'd still be there if I wanted, but busy. Slower to reply. There were all the other stations, of course. Thirty people direct and hundreds more in the Sphere. But there was someone else I probably should send a message to. I'd been putting that off. I wanted to wait until it wasn't just one long angry screed, because even I knew anger wasn't fair. No one stayed forever in real life. Nothing lasted.

We'd parted in silence and fury. Her absence still ached.

I swiped the camera off the screen, brought up the long-distance comms hub and the proper keyboard. This was going to need both hands and all my attention.

"Dear Noa. I hope you're enjoying your retirement. I miss you but I'm getting used to the quiet."

I paused as I considered what to say, what to tell this person who had once known everything that happened. That gave me my answer.

"You won't believe what happened today..."

Louise Hughes is a speculative fiction writer from the North East of England. She is also a time traveller, likes to be at the top of mountains, and knits more jumpers than she realistically needs. Her work has appeared in *Strange Horizons, Daily Science Fiction* and *Interzone.*
Louise Hughes is neurodivergent.

Superheroes
Kaitlin Pradhan

I think a lot of people can relate to superheroes in some way. For me, particularly the characters from the live-action DC TV shows 'Supergirl', 'The Flash' and 'Superman and Lois', they're often the only characters on screen that look like me.

Being autistic is often a lot like having superpowers because I can see, hear and feel the world in ways that neurotypical people can't. And these characters know exactly what having superpowers is like, if in the more literal sense. They know what it's like to be afraid of what they can do, to hide their powers because others don't accept them for it, to live in a world where having these superpowers isn't always easy.

But they also know what it's like to live in a world that needs them, where their superpowers are the very thing that can save the world. These characters have shown me that my superpowers are my strengths, that I can be proud of and confident in, who I am. But the superheroes and other characters from these shows have also shown me that the most important superpowers are things that anyone can have – hope and kindness.

I love the futuristic worlds these characters live in, the technology they use, and the way their characters' passion allows them to hyper-fixate on things, like science and creating

gadgets, in order to save lives and change the world.

But I wish we didn't have to wait for the future for these characters to be seen in the real world. Because here's the thing.

I'm not a superhero. And I don't live in a world with aliens, spaceships and literal superpowers.

I'm a human girl. From planet Earth. I'm not invincible, I can't stop a train, when I fall I bleed, and kryptonite is not a green stone that powerful villains get their hands on – it's the overwhelming stimulation when I leave the house that can make me feel like I'm drowning; it's the sensation of touching sequins where every sparkle feels like a blade being driven into my skin.

My biggest fear isn't about someone finding out about my secret identity. It's for all those who are like me, who shouldn't have to go through life unseen, just because the world isn't built to see us.

Superheroes may know what it's like to literally save the world with their powers. But there's also a lot that they don't know.

They don't know what it's like to feel music in colours, to feel such emotion in hearing every instrument and seeing every colour of the rainbow reflected before their eyes as the chorus strikes. They don't know the indescribable calm and peace that comes from standing outside in nature or being with animals, the way the natural colours soothe, the way the leaves whisper their reassurance, the way the wind blows all worries away, the way that animals love without judgement and speak without words.

Superheroes don't know the feeling of frustration when they can't communicate, not because they can't communicate their secret identity, but because they can't communicate at all to tell someone they like their hair or ask them how their weekend was, simply because the neurotypical world moves too fast for them to do so. Superheroes don't know the feeling as if they're standing in golden rays of light when non-verbal communication is seen as valid as verbal words, when they can say their opinion and be heard, when someone asks them to join in, or if they need a break, or just say hi. They don't know the excitement and the delight that can be experienced that is so great that the only way to express it is to jump up and down or flap their hands and vocalise.

I wish that characters who looked like me on screen weren't so because they came from a distant, alien planet, or were involved in some freak accident. I wish they looked like me because they're human, because their neurodivergence is human, because their stories are important and deserve to be told. Because my community needs their voices to be heard, to be listened to. Because the positive, accurate representation of neurodivergence onscreen can literally change lives. And that is what's going to save the world.

Kaitlin is an autistic writer with synaesthesia who wants to empower autistic youth and help make the world a more accepting and understanding place, by sharing her stories. She is based in Perth, Australia and writes about magic, fantasy and being autistic.

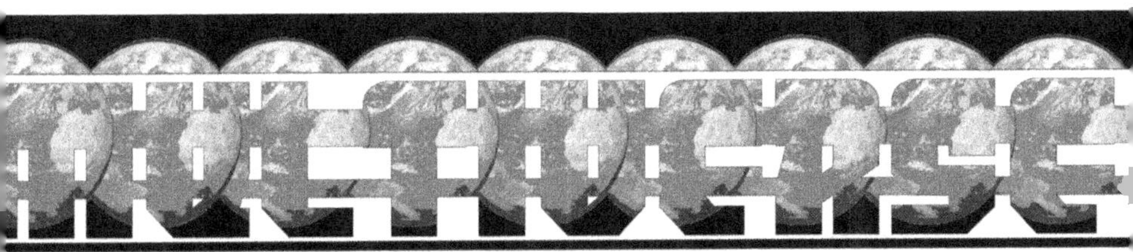

I Landed Here

When you land on Earth
You have to use mirrors
So your mouth matches theirs
And your eyes go with it.

They tell you that
Being like them
Is for you. It's not.
It's for them.

When you land on Earth
You have to use their tools
Learn to tie laces, ride bikes.
Even if they laugh at you.

They tell you that
They like you
As you, but only when
You're like them.

When you land on Earth
You acclimatise to the fabrics
Some of them scratch, or burn,
But they're supposed to.

They tell you that
Everyone's a little odd
They're not;
Not like you.

I landed here
Thirty years ago.
This guidebook is incomplete.
More research required.

A. P. Slevin

The Meeting of the Martians

The earth shook, and Martians came out
of nowhere. I had never seen a Martian before.
They sure looked funny to me, and they had never
seen humans before. We looked at each other –
you know what Martians look like? Flying saucers.
They see flying saucers in outer space.

Martians are on this Earth. They inhabit the
Earth, along with humans. What do Martians call
humans? Maybe Martians call humans Humanoids?

What do Martians eat?
The earth shook again. I got frightened and screamed and ran
as fast as my feet would go. The Martians kept following me.
They kept running after me.

All of a sudden, I woke up in a sweat, crying and
hugging my husband in a tight squeeze.
The Martians were following me in my dream. It was
a bad dream... or *was* it just a dream?

Looking out at the window, seeing the clouds,
I see clouds in my coffee. What are the clouds in my
coffee? Is it steam coming out?
I know that there are not really clouds in my coffee...

I like the dream about Martians... here they come again.
There are a lot of them. They are running after me.
"Stop!" I yell at them... I put my hand out to try to get them to
stop. The Martians keep following me. They try to be nice to me.
I try to be nice back to them. They *are* nice. I share my coffee
with the Martians. They like the coffee. I share my sandwich with them.
The Martians, what do they share with me? They share a Mars Bar with me:
a candy bar from Mars! They share a Mars Bar with me – that is all
    Martians have
eaten until now. We get to know each other. Then the Martians disappear
    into the clouds and
go away. I go my separate direction, too. Until we meet again.

Amy Rosenfield-Kass

Amy lives in New York and continues to be happily married after three and
a half years. She likes adventure, fun, to be happy, and likes to travel with her
husband. She has been taking a variety of art classes, and likes mixed media,
writing and being creative. Amy has authored a book, *Daniel and Max Play
Together* – she was asked to adapt the book to go along with the PBS episode,
Daniel and Max Play Together.
She works part time, as a school librarian and helps children with reading,
writing and literacy.
Amy's advice: Just write, try, and don't be afraid to write.

In Sims, capitalism doesn't mean we all end up dead

There is a cheat
code that
doesn't require you
to be an asshole
but we still don't need
it. We eat avocado
toast and smile
all day. I get fat
with your love
and walk the
black lab every
half an hour. We
buy you that
easel and I make
money off my
novel and I still
have time to
pet the dog.
We finally have
that baby and I
am not
suicidal and
we are not
poor.

Elspeth Wilson

Elspeth Wilson is a writer and poet who is interested in exploring the limitations and possibilities of the body through writing.
They identify as both disabled and neurodivergent. Their poems have been nominated for Best of the Net and commended in Young Poets' Network challenges and their prose has been shortlisted for Canongate's Nan Shepherd prize and Penguin's Write Now Editorial programme.
Elspeth is currently working on their debut collection and also regularly facilitates accessible creative workshops. When they aren't writing or reading, they can usually be found near the sea or spending time with their elderly dog.

Content Notes

The Apology – unhealthy relationships, detailed violent fantasies, systemically abusive capitalist dystopia, poverty, ableist jokes, media misogyny, panic and fawn responses due to emotional abuse, gross negligence manslaughter and displacement.

A Burden Eased – legalised home invasion, threat of death, media misogyny, systemically abusive capitalist dystopia, sexual harassment, callous descriptions of injury and death in war, systemic ageist murder, brief mention of assisted dying, ableism, killing oneself as a form of protest.

Glue Guns in Paradise – police (but not as we know them), threat of knife violence, psychosis, germaphobia, attempted stabbing, physical restraint (but less harmful than we know it), non-consensual medical treatments, mention of homelessness.

How Yer Glaikit Gran Beat Back the Beat – impending death, mention of alcoholism, poverty, graverobbing, cybernetic infection.

The Alien Invasion – domestic violence, head injury, neglect, implied alcoholism, seizure, chronic pain, brain injury, mentions of bullying and ableism.

Relay – isolated living conditions, abandonment issues, intruders, distress from disrupted routines and systems, attempted theft, false accusations.

Superheroes – discussion of anti-autistic ableism and media representation issues.

I Landed Here – masking, ableism, sensory difficulties.

In Sims, capitalism doesn't mean we all end up dead – pregnancy, suicidality, poverty.